KV-245-192

Lea Bakes an Apple Pie Surprise

WITHDRAWN
FROM
STOCK

by Jay Dale

illustrated by Amanda Gulliver

"Dad," said Lea.

"I can see lots of big red apples on the tree.

Can we bake an apple pie for Grandma?"

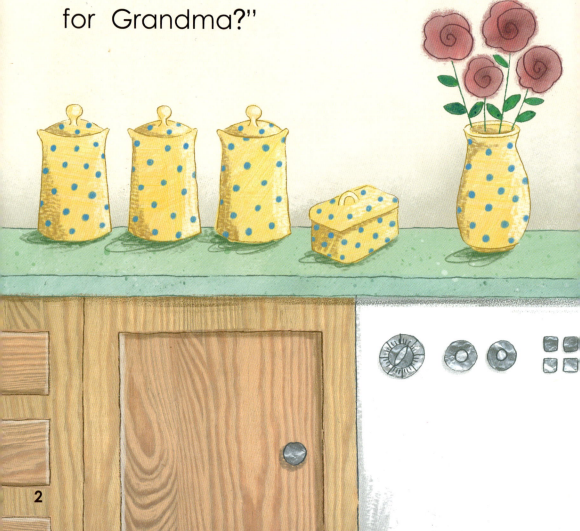

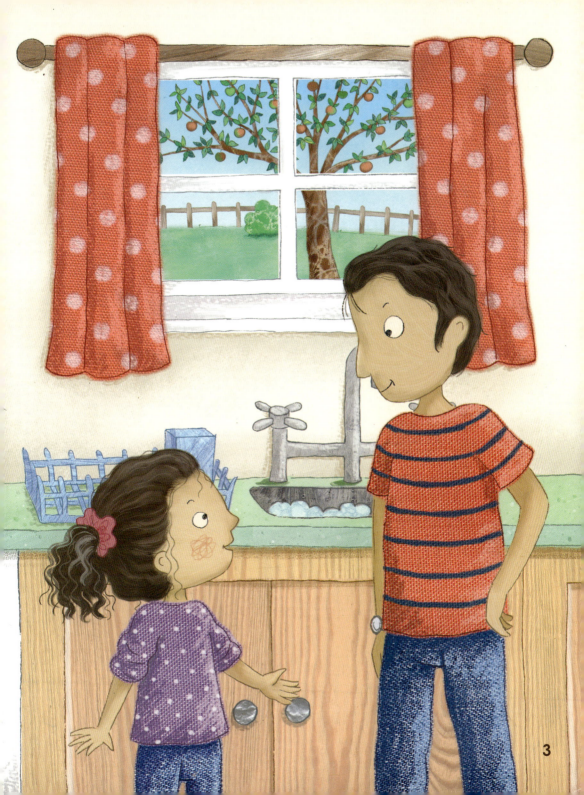

"Yes," said Dad.

"Grandma will be here today."

"Oh, good!" said Lea.

"The apple pie can be a surprise."

Dad got a ladder from the shed.
Lea got a basket.

"Up you go, Lea!" said Dad.

Lea went up the ladder.
She got 4 big red apples.

Lea and Dad went into the house.

"Here is a bowl,"
said Lea.
"The milk goes in.
The flour goes in.
The butter goes in too!"

Mix! Mix! Mix!

9

Dad cut up the apples.

Chop! Chop! Chop!

"Here is a big pot,"
said Dad.
"The apples and sugar
go in the big pot."

Bubble! Bubble! Bubble!

"The apples can go in the pie,"
said Lea.

Plop! Plop! Plop!

"The pie can go in the oven," said Dad.

"The pie looks good," said Lea.

"Oh!" cried Lea.

"Grandma is here!

The pie can come out!"

"Surprise!" shouted Lea.

"We baked you an apple pie."

"Oh!" said Grandma.

"Thank you! I love apple pie.

And I love surprises too!"